W9-APK-808

For Aaron
—LL

SIMON AND SCHUSTER BOOKS FOR YOUNG READERS
Simon & Schuster Building, Rockefeller Center, 1230 Avenue of the Americas, New York, New York 10020

Copyright © 1990 by Lee Lorenz. All rights reserved including the right of reproduction in whole or in part in any form. SIMON AND SCHUSTER BOOKS FOR YOUNG READERS is a trademark of Simon & Schuster Inc. Manufactured in the United States of America.

10 9 8 7 6 5 4 3 2 1
Library of Congress Cataloging-in-Publication Data
Lorenz, Lee. Dinah's egg. Summary: A cumulative series of slapstick near-disasters befalls a dinosaur egg before it lands safely in its mother's nest in time to hatch. [1. Eggs—Fiction. 2. Dinosaurs—Fiction.] I. Title.
PZ7.L884Di 1990 [E]—dc20 89-35481
ISBN 0-671-68685-2

DINAH'S EGG

written and illustrated by Lee Lorenz

SIMON AND SCHUSTER BOOKS FOR YOUNG READERS
Published by Simon and Schuster Inc., New York

Many long years ago, a dinosaur named Dinah sat on her nest, patiently waiting for her egg to hatch.

Suddenly, great storm clouds rolled across the sky.
Thunder crashed and lightning splintered the inky
black clouds.

Rain fell, the wind howled, and the earth shook so hard
that Dinah's egg popped right out of the nest.

Downhill it rolled, splashing through puddles and startling salamanders until it dropped over the edge of a cliff.

Down and down it plunged, only to land in the branches of a dead tree. From nearby, a giant spotted snake watched with greedy eyes.

What a tasty morsel, he thought as he drew himself up
the tree toward Dinah's egg.

But the tree was too weak to hold the giant snake. As the tree's roots pulled free, the greedy snake dropped into the canyon, but the egg rolled off the branches to safety on the far side of the canyon. Faster and faster the egg rolled down the hillside until…

...it dropped straight toward the smiling jaws
of a crocodile.

But the monster's jaws snapped shut on nothing as a great bird swooped out of the sky and carried Dinah's egg off in its claws.

I've never hatched a blue *egg before*, she thought, as she flew toward her nest. Just then a final bolt of lightning singed her tail feathers, and she dropped the egg.

Over and over the egg turned as it plunged down
through clouds of steam toward the center of a boiling
volcano.

But as white-hot lava seemed to reach up for Dinah's egg, a rising gas bubble softly cradled it and carried it gently away.

The bubble drifted up, away from the volcano and over a distant ridge, where it popped as it grazed the top of a thorn tree.

Once more the egg was falling, this time splashing
down in a stream that carried it swiftly toward a
roaring waterfall.

As Dinah's egg floated over
the falls toward the boulders
below, a giant fish leaped from
the water and swallowed it
in one gulp.

With the egg floating in its belly, the fish swam downstream.

Suddenly, powerful claws slashed through the waves.

A giant lizard knocked the fish out of the water and
Dinah's egg out of the fish.

The egg tumbled through
the air, fell into a hollow
log, rolled through the log,
dropped onto a sleeping
stegosaurus, bumped over
his spiny back, flew off
again, and…

...dropped into the nest
of a cranky old millipede.
"As if I didn't have
enough trouble keeping
this place clean," grumbled
the millipede.

He drew himself up and kicked the egg with as many
legs as he could without falling down.

The egg shot out of the hole like a rocket, flew
gracefully through the air, and...

…landed softly back in Dinah's nest.

Dinah couldn't believe her eyes. As she bent down for a
closer look, the egg began to crack open.

A fuzzy little head pushed out through the shell, blinked, and cried, "Mama!" Dinah covered her baby with a big welcoming kiss.

Dinah's egg was home.